C.N. McCormick

The Queen City of the South. Natchez, Mississippi

C.N. McCormick

The Queen City of the South. Natchez, Mississippi

ISBN/EAN: 9783337325077

Printed in Europe, USA, Canada, Australia, Japan

Cover: Foto ©Andreas Hilbeck / pixelio.de

More available books at **www.hansebooks.com**

The Queen City of the South.

NATCHEZ, MISSISSIPPI

On Top, not "Under the Hill."

Its Beautiful and Healthy Location, the Superior Facilities
for Manufactories and the Low Cost of Living Justify
the Assertion that Health, Happiness and
Wealth Awaits All Good Citizens.

ADAMS COUNTY

And the Neighboring Territory,

With Fertile Soil, Suitable for the Cultivation of any Crop
Known to the North, and Many Unknown There
Contribute to Natchez' Prosperity.

NATCHEZ:
DAILY DEMOCRAT STEAM PRINT.

PREFACE.

Knowledge of the idea which prevails in the North, East and West that the Southern people do not welcome strangers in their midst has prompted this work. It has been the aim of the editor to present unvarnished facts for the consideration of those into whose hands this pamphlet may fall, and we send it forth dedicating it to the welfare of the merchants who have so generously aided its publication, and of the whole country it represents.

An incident in connection with this publication will suffice to illustrate the feeling of our people: The editor is an Ohioan, who, after a residence of almost two years here, conceived the idea of telling the "up-country" people something of this portion of the Sunny South and thought to attract attention by the title "Points to the Yankees." It did attract attention, but at the wrong end of the line. A number of most prominent citizens at once objected saying: "We like your idea, but your title, never! The epithet 'Yankee' was applied in time of war, with all hatred, and was intended as a mortal insult to our invading enemies. But that time has long since passed, and, sir, WE ARE ALL YANKEES NOW.' This same feeling pervades the whole community in and around Natchez to an extent that is almost universally observed by strangers, and that makes a residence here, from the very first, a pleasant one There is no section of the South or North where the stranger is sooner or more pleasantly made to feel at home.

Many of the articles are contributions of genuine Southerners who are well known for their integrity, their familiarity with the history and growth of Natchez and the country tributary thereto, the customs and feelings of the people; and what they have to say may be relied on. We return thanks to the contributors for their kind assistance, and hope they may live to see our beautiful city reap the harvest they have sown.

The NATCHEZ DAILY DEMOCRAT and corps have placed us under obligations for innumerable and valuable favors, for which we are gratified to thus publicly thank them.

The illustrations are all good for which due credit should be given to Mr. H. C. Norman, photographer, of this city, and Messrs. A. Zeese & Co., engravers, Chicago.

G. N. M'CORMICK.

[ESTABLISHED 1865.]

THE NATCHEZ DEMOCRAT

——[Daily and Weekly.]——

OFFICIAL ORGAN OF THE CITY AND COUNTY.

JAMES W. LAMBERT, Proprietor.

SUBSCRIPTION PRICE:

Daily, $9.00 Per Year, in Advance.
Weekly, $1.50 Per Year, in Advance.

THE DEMOCRAT'S

JOB DEPARTMENT

——IS SUPPLIED WITH——

EVERYTHING NECESSARY FOR FIRST-CLASS WORK

BILL HEADS,   CIRCULARS,   POSTERS,
NOTE HEADS,   PROGRAMMES,   DODGERS,
LETTER HEADS,   INVITATIONS.   Etc., Etc., Etc.

ORDERS BY MAIL WILL RECEIVE PROMPT ATTENTION.

THIS PAMPHLET IS A SPECIMEN OF OUR WORK.

NATCHEZ:
ITS PAST, PRESENT AND FUTURE.

BY MAJ. THOMAS GRAFTON,
EDITOR NATCHEZ DEMOCRAT.

THE City of Natchez is 272 miles above New Orleans, on the Mississippi river, and is one of the oldest towns in the Southwest. The site for the town was selected by Bienville in 1700, and the fortress of Fort Rosalie was erected and settlers brought to the place in 1712, two years before the same indomitable chieftain located the City of New Orleans. The magnificent beauty of the location attracted the attention of the adventurous explorer after encountering the gloomy monotony of three hundred miles of travel on the muddy river, through swamps covered with a dense growth of timber hung with the sombre and funereal Spanish moss, and dense jungles of cane, palmetto and thickets of undergrowth.

Bienville at once located a site for a town on the romantic hills which here at an elevation of nearly two hundred feet overlook the channel of the mightiest river in the world. He doubtless designed it as the place for the seat of government of the French of d'Iberville, but the latter, a few years later, fixed his government at New Orleans and Natchez was garrisoned and held as an outpost of the new French settlement. The fort called Rosalie in honor of the beautiful countess of Ponchartrain, and Natchez derived its name from the tribe of Indians which inhabited the country in the vicinity of the fortress. Tradition points to this tribe as one of the most intelligent of all the aboriginal tribes and romance has painted them in colors that scarcely correspond with our ideas of the modern Indian savage. Count de Chateaubriand, who, at a later period, traveled in this section of the country, doubtless heard these romantic traditions of the Natchez, and these together with the beautiful landscapes and the grand scenery of the country around Natchez doubtless

MAJOR THOMAS GRAFTON.

inspired the lovely episode of "Attala," inserted in his wonderful work *Genie du Christianisme*, and the characteristic descriptions in "The Natchez" and "Rene."

The French garrison soon alienated the good opinions of the Natchez and it was not long before they conspired with other tribes for its destruction. Tradition says a daughter of the "Sun," the chief of the Natchez, who loved one of the officers of the garrison, endeavored to save the French from their fate, but in vain. She succeeded, however, in so deranging the plans of the Indians that only her own tribe, the Natchez, were present on the day fixed for the massacre. These, under the pretense of having a grand ball play, assembled around the Fort, the large entrance to which was left open that the garrison might witness the sports of the Indians. In the midst of the play one of the Indians sent the ball flying through the open gate, and there was a general rush of the dusky players through the gate as if to recover the ball. Having thus gained entrance to the Fort, and the French suspecting no danger, an attack was made on the defenceless soldiers and soon most of them fell victims to the revenge of the Indians.

This massacre, which occurred in 1729, was soon after avenged by the French and the Indian tribes who had now become the enemies of their former allies, the Natchez, and this most interesting of all the Southern Indian tribes, was exterminated. The name of the lost tribe was, however retained as that of the new settlement, and the "Natchez country" soon became noted for its beauty and fertility, and it was soon one of the most flourishing of the French-American settlements. It continued to be a French military and trading post until 1763 when it passed by treaty into the hands of the English. The name of the

Fort was changed to Panmure. Scarcely a vestige of its history remains during its posses-sion by England, but a number of English settlers came to the place, the descendants of a few of whom still remain among the population.

In the year 1779 it was taken possession of by Spain as a part of Florida, and contin-ued under Spanish control until 1797, when a rectification of the lines between the United States and the Spanish colonies threw it into the United States.

The occupation of Natchez by the Spanish government is probably the most interesting period of its early history. Large numbers of enterprising Americans, attracted by the fame of the fertility and beauty of the country, and encouraged by the generous manner in which they were treated by the Spanish regime, flocked to Natchez and its vicinity, and long before it was known to be American territory the anglicised population were prepared for the advent of a Republican form of government.

The residence of the Spanish Governor was at Natchez, and for the greater part of the time of the Spanish administration the position was held by Don Manuel Gayoso de Lemos, ably assisted by Don Stephen Minor, an American who had taken service with Spain. Gov-ernor Gayoso was a man of liberal views and encouraged the immigration of settlers from

NATCHEZ CITY HOSPITAL.

every country, to whom he willingly made grants of land for settlement and lots in the city for building. He anticipated a brilliant future for the seat of his government. The resi-dence lots of the various classes of settlers in the town were kept pretty strictly separated, and that portion near the bluffs on the river was known to the settlers as "Spanish Town," while that portion east of the present Commerce street was designated "Irish Town." It is related that a rather well to-do man, not of Spanish origin, approached the Governor with a request for a building lot near the bluffs. "No, sir," was the Governor's reply; "No, sir. This part of the City is reserved for the residences of Spanish Grandees."

A Church was erected in what was intended to be the centre of the town and from the door of this Church the town was laid off in rectangular squares embracing within the city one mile in each direction. All the lands in this boundary were donated in lots to settlers, except the space "reserved for the residences of Spanish Grandees," which fell into the hands of the United States government and afterwards became the source of bitter litigation between the City and Jefferson College.

The buildings in the town were of an humble and rather primitive character, and few traces of them are now in existence.

At length the United States took active steps to settle the question of the limits of the

two countries, as it was evident that the claim of Spain was made to territory far north of its true boundary. A detachment of troops under command of Capt. Guion was sent to demand possession of Natchez in 1797. The detachment consisted of two companies of infantry selected from the command of General (Mad Anthony) Wayne and were commanded by Lieuts. Pope and McCleary. After considerable delay, during which a good deal of excitement existed among the American inhabitants, negotiations were brought to an end by the silent withdrawal, at night, of the Spanish troops, and the United States flag was peacefully hoisted over the ramparts of Fort Panmure, and Natchez was recognized as an American town. In 1798 Mississippi was organized as a Territory, and Natchez was made the Capital. Hon. Winthrop Sargent, the first Governor, had his residence here, and with his Executive Council framed the laws for the Territory.

As in the present day, the printing press followed the footsteps of American pioneers, and probably the first newspaper ever printed in the Southwest was issued in Natchez by Col. Andrew Murschalk, in 1798. The first laws for the regulation of the Territory were printed by him the same year.

After the transfer of the Territory, immigration to Natchez and its vicinity became rapid and the town soon assumed a prosperous and thriving appearance; soon the log and picket houses were replaced by brick and frame tenements. The trade of the place in-

PROTESTANT ORPHAN ASYLUM.

creased rapidly, and the foundations of large fortunes were laid by commercial men in Natchez. Millaudom, of New Orleans, Mullanphy, of St. Louis, Ralston, of Philadelphia, Washington Jackson, of Liverpool, and many other prominent merchants of the United States and other countries began their mercantile career in Natchez. Probably in no part of the United States was wealth more rapidly accumulated than it was by the hardy and adventurous men who were the pioneers in the American settlement of Natchez.

The soil of the country contiguous to the City was of an extremely fertile character and the cultivation of cotton by slave labor was exceedingly profitable, and the planter who gave proper attention to his business soon became wealthy, and the merchants of the town found a large sale for their goods at very remunerative profits. The first forty years of the present century was the most prosperous period in the history of Natchez, and the wealth and enterprise of its people were at least equal to that of any community in the United States.

Early in this century a branch of the United States Bank was established in Natchez, and a State bank, the Bank of Mississippi, was also established in 1809. With these the business of the merchants and others of the town and surrounding country was conducted, and they were the only banking institutions in the State until 1830, when the Planters' Bank was chartered to take the place of the Mississippi Bank whose charter was about to expire.

About this time a speculative mania began in the States and it was found that the banking facilities of the City were not sufficient for its business demands. The Agricultural Bank was chartered and not long after another, the Commercial Bank, was added to the number, and at the same time banking privileges were conferred upon a Railroad Company incorporated for the construction of a road from Natchez to Jackson, and the Natchez Shipping Company, organized for direct shipping between the port of Natchez and the ports of the world.

A cotton compress was built, and in 1838 as many as six sailing vessels of good size were lying at one time at the wharf near the compress loading with cotton for the East and for England. About the same time probably the first cotton seed oil mill ever built was constructed in this city. The process of linting and hulling the seed, and of purifying the oil was unknown to these adventurous oil men and a market for their crude oil could not be found, and financial troubles prevented them from realizing the benefits of their enterprise.

A cotton mill was also erected about the same time, and thus Natchez had at that early date, three of the enterprises which fifty years after have been found to be so profitable, and one, a direct shipping enterprise, which has not yet been revived.

In 1836 or '37 the people of Natchez began the construction of a railroad, of a 5-feet

ROSALIE COTTON MILL.

gauge, to Jackson, and finished it some forty miles on a perfectly level grade, it being tho't at that time that a locomotive could not overcome any serious grade. It, too, was stopped by the financial troubles which followed a period of inflation.

It has already been said that during the decade from 1830 to 1840 Natchez had five banks of issue and deposit. During the same period some twenty-five banks were chartered and put in operation in other places in the State. These all discounted largely while very few of them had any considerable line of deposits. A speculative mania had seized upon the people of Mississippi in which those of Natchez largely shared. A personal endorsement, generally not of a gilt-edged character, was all that was necessary to secure loans at easy rates from the banks. A redundancy of currency naturally produced inflation in value of real estate, and plantations and slaves were bought and sold at extravagant prices. This continued until the country was filled with irredeemable currency, and finally the bubble burst bringing ruin upon those who bought at inflated prices.

It may be imagined that the business of the City received a severe check from the reduction of values to one-tenth of what they had before been. Wide-spread ruin was the result and a blow had been given to all kinds of business from which under the most favorable circumstances it would have been hard to recover.

To add to the depression: in May, 1840, Natchez was visited by one of the most de-

structive tornados that has ever occurred in this country. Its business houses were leveled with the ground and the whole city was a wreck. From this blow, under the depressed condition of financial matters, the City was very slow in recovering.

The planters, in the meanwhile, had formed business connections in distant cities and the plantation business of the City was reduced to a minimum. Planting was found to be the most profitable business, and investments were made almost entirely in cotton planting, the planters making their purchases almost entirely in New Orleans, Cincinnati, St. Louis and other distant cities. All the banks failed, the compress, the oil mill, the cotton factory, and even the railroad had to succumb to the stringency of the financial condition.

Thus Natchez, from being one of the leading towns in the South, became secondary in importance, and although it was always valued as a place of residence, on account of its beautiful location, its healthy climate, the excellence of its public school system, and the high morality that characterized its people; it lost much of its prestige and the war coming on gave a final blow to its old time prosperity.

When the war closed it was for a while thought the City could never recover from the ruin which had been brought upon the people of Natchez and its vicinity. The wealth of the planters was gone, and those who had lived a life of luxury and elegance found themselves reduced to poverty.

But the war which had spread ruin and desolation over the land, had left to Natchez a

Residence of R. F. Learned, President Natchez Cotton Mills Company.

class of earnest, enterprising young men who went to work vigorously to recruit their fortunes. Their service in the army had accustomed them to work and hardened their sinews and prepared their hearts for the struggle in a more peaceful field, for an object not less dear to them, the comfort and support of themselves and their families. With brave hearts they worked at the task of building a new prosperity on the ruins which they found left to them by the unfortunate contest through which they had just passed. The results have been such as the most sanguine among them could scarcely have hoped for.

As the South has been rehabilitated under the changed condition of our labor system, so Natchez too has put on a new phase, and one which promises to make of it a more prosperous and important City than it has ever been before. Probably no locality in the South passed through the era of reconstruction more quietly and more prudently than Natchez. By the tact of its people the City and County government was restored to its intelligent people without a single act of violence or one drop of blood shed. Quietly and peacefully the control of public affairs was regained and the class of population from whom danger was feared acquiesced in the action of our prudent citizens with apparent pleasure.

With the restoration of the City and County governments to intelligent and honest hands, one of the first things was the construction of a railroad from Natchez to Jackson, a point where connection was formed with the system of railroads extending in every direction over the Union.   This work was done by home capital alone, the County issuing its bonds which were taken by citizens of the County, for the construction of this road

This gave the first impulse to a spirit of enterprise which speedily resulted in the erection of two large cotton mills, two mills for the manufacture of cotton seed oil, two iron foundries, a cotton compress, an elevator from the river to the top of the high bluff on which the City stands, a street railway and a large number of minor manufacturing establishments.

It is the proud boast of the people of Natchez that it has depended for its improvements solely on the enterprise of its own people.   Its isolated position had prevented it from attracting the attention of the capitalists of the world, and in self defense it was compelled to be self dependent.

The spirited action of its people has now however, drawn attention to it, and enterprises are being projected which will add very largely to its commercial importance.   One of the most important of these is a railroad on which work will be begun early in the fall, the New Orleans, Natchez & Fort Scott railroad, which connects Natchez directly with the Great West and makes it a distributing point for Northern products to a very large portion of the Southwest.

The extension of the Natchez, Jackson & Columbus railroad to Columbus and Decatur, which is a probability of the near future, will make one of the most direct outlets to the Mississippi river for the rich mineral productions of Alabama and Tennessee.

FIRST NATIONAL BANK OF NATCHEZ.

A road has also been built with Natchez capital from Vidalia, La., to Trinity, on Black river, which will doubtless develope into a western road through Texas and give to Natchez the benefit of one of the best trades in the South.   In addition to these roads, a railroad is contemplated due east from Natchez through the finest forests of pine timber in the United States, which, when built would bring here for shipment immense quantities of lumber for the North and West.

These and other railroad enterprises that are in contemplation, will make of this City a centre of trade that will be surpassed by no other city in the South.   The manufacturing spirit of the people of Natchez, together with its facilities for carrying on industries of all kinds, points to the conclusion that it will become one of the most important of Southern manufacturing cities.

These all indicate a future for Natchez that will be brilliant and useful.   Its beautiful location, its delightful climate, its phenomenal healthfulness, the fertility of the country which surrounds it, the generosity and hospitality of its people all point to Natchez and its vicinity at the present time as it did in the years long ago, as the garden of the South, the favorite land of the emigrant hunting a home, of the invalid in search of health, and of the denizen of the bleak, cold North seeking a genial winter home in a land of sunny homes and generous hearts.

GOVERNMENT AND POLITICS.

THE Municipal Government of Natchez is simple and inexpensive. The Executive and Legislative government is vested in a Mayor and Board of eight Aldermen. Two aldermen represent the people of each ward, and they are elected on alternate years for a term of two years each.

HON. WM. H. MALLERY, Mayor.

The working force of the Board is constituted by committees, appointed by the Mayor.

The Board elect all the subordinate officers, city clerk, assessor, treasurer, solicitor, marshal and police force.

The Mayor is ex-officio Recorder and judge of the Police court, and has jurisdiction in all cases coming under the city ordinances.

JOHN GRADY, Alderman, 1st Ward.

City monies are closely looked after by the Finance committee of the Board, and the streets, Fires, Lights, Water, Health, and other committees, keeps the corporation in a healthy state financially and physically.

Annually, in August, the committees make up their budget of probable expenses for the ensuing year, and make the tax levy just cover it.

The city debt is small only $18,000 in warrants which are receivable at par for city taxes, so there is no necessity for a sinking

L. G. ALDRICH, Alderman, 1st Ward.

fund, consequently taxes are low.

Politics might be said to be unknown here, the tickets rarely if ever contain the name of a party, or, if they do, it is not read. The people, white and black, look out for the interest of the city and vote for the individual they will best fill the position to which he aspires.

OUR SCHOOLS.

BY PROF. J. W. HENDERSON, SUPERINTENDENT.

THE public schools of Natchez are one of its interesting features; and the liberal scale upon which they are conducted is a striking evidence of the hold which they have upon the hearts of her citizens. Enrolled in these schools are 1195 pupils, distributed as follows: White, males, 269; white females, 286; colored males, 276; colored females, 367. Twenty-three teachers are employed at salaries ranging from $40 to $100 per month. The school session commences October 1, and continues nine months, leaving a vacation during the months of July, August and September. Separate buildings are provided for the two races; these are large, well ventilated, well lighted and are located in different quarters of the city. Play-grounds, maps, blackboards, abundance of fuel in winter, and everything that can conduce to the moral, intellectual and physical welfare of the children, are liberally provided. The school for whites is divided into twelve departments; that for blacks into eleven departments. Each school has its principal and both are under the supervision of a general superintendent.

The school for whites has been in existence more than forty years. Many of our

GEO. T. PAYNE, Alderman, 2d Ward.

most substantial citizens are indebted to it alone for the education which has made them influential men in our community, and to-day it is as thorough and systematic as it has ever been in the past.

There are also a number of private schools

P. W. MULVIHILL, Alderman, 2d Ward.

in the city for small children, and one or two normal institutions where the higher branches are taught.

Natchez college, an advanced institution,

for colored people, is located in the suburbs of the city, and is successfully managed.

At Washington six miles away is old Jefferson College. one of the oldest institutions of its kind in the United States. Jefferson Davis, the famous president of the Confederacy was a student there, and associated with him were some of the greatest statesmen Mississippi has produced. The college is liberally endowed and gives a very thorough course.

OUR INDUSTRIES.

WHEN you begin to talk of manufactories, the South takes a seat several rows from the front, Nevertheless she is an interested spectator and is fast

J. B. O'BRIEN, Alderman, 3d Ward.

working forward. In the olden times, from sheer force of habit, she looked northward for every manufactured article ; even sending all her great cotton product to the eastern mills to be worked up into cloth, thinking, doubtless, that the number of mills in that part of the country was sufficient to supply all demands likely ever to be made upon them, and that to put money into a mill in the South was next thing to throwing it into the fire; then, too, they were a fastidious people. and did not like the idea of having the privacy of their beautiful homes invaded by the smoke and dust and noise which are attendant upon great manufactories. Years, and increasing population and demands, proved their error however, and they were not slow to see that if the

South would prosper she must subordinate pride to necessity and industry.

With the balance Natchez sized up the situation and went to work. As a result we show.

The Natchez Cotton Mill, which occupies nearly a whole block in the city, with handsome buildings, where over three hundred persons are employed, running three hundred looms and ten thousand spindles, where over

A. L. HOWE, Alderman, 3d Ward.

$4,000 per month are paid out in wages, where about 4,000 bales of cotton are consumed annually in making about 5,000,000 yards of cloth.

The Rosalie Mills another industry in the same line, where over 3,000 bales of cotton are annually manufactured into towels, blue

R. S. DIXON, Alderman, 4th Ward.

cloth and a variety of other grades of goods, where $3,000 are monthly paid to employes.

Two large Cotton Seed Oil Mills, employing about seventy-five men each The works of these institutions occupy nearly two blocks, and are a portion of the greatest industrial enterprise ever started in the South.

A Cotton Compress, where bales of the great staple are placed in the most compact form for foreign shipment. This new enterprises has probably done the city more good than the same investment ever did any town. It has brought this year over 15,000 bales of cotton to this market more than usual. It has made this a point where buyers congregate, and the prices paid during

GEO. T. REHN, Alderman, 4th Ward.

the past season have compared most favorably with New Orleans.

Two Brass and Iron Foundries, one of them an extensive institution, employing a large number of skilled mechanics and en-

THOS. R. QUARTERMAN, City Clerk.

tering extensively into the manufacture of steam boilers and engines.

Two Cotton Gins of large capacity, using steam power, and employing many hands each.

A Batting Mill where the lint from the cotton seed is manufactured into neat rolls of cotton batting which are shipped North to be used in making comforts to protect the people from King Frost on cold nights.

Two Extensive Lumber Mills, supplying the demand for building material, in native woods.

An Ice Factory, with a capacity of eighteen tons every twenty-four hours.

The Bluff City Railway company with wharf and incline to the hill tops and tracks through the city for the distribution of freight,

F. J. Arrighi, City Assessor.

is a convenient and paying institution and employs usually about forty men.

A Stained Glass Works is about ready to open business, and is the first of its kind in the South. It is started by two of our most energetic young men associated with a gen-

W. T. MARTIN, Pres. N. J. & C. Ry.

tleman from the North, and its prospects are of the finest.

A Street Railway traverses the city from the steamboat landing to a park two and a half miles away in the eastern suburbs of the

city, and gives employment to ten or twelve men.

The manner of receiving our coal supply makes this a great industry. The coal comes here from the upper Ohio in barges and has to be wheeled out onto the bank in barrows which gives employment to three hundred men at least six months in the year.

Two Brick Yards, each owning extensive

S. E. RUMBLE, Pres. Bluff City Ry.

grounds and manufacturing first-class goods at reasonable prices, are among the great wage-paying industries of our city.

Two mineral water bottling establishments with a capacity each of 180 dozen bottles.

Three manufacturing confectioners, two of whom make 1200 pounds of candy per

THOS. REBER, Pres. Natchez Street Ry.

day each, and give employment to eight or ten men.

A meal mill in connection with one of the gins does the local grinding.

A beer bottling institution of large capacity.

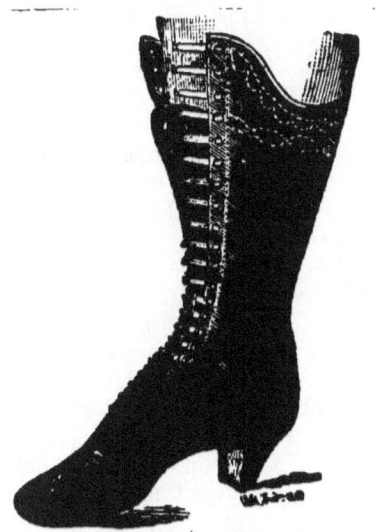

There are also in course of construction a fine system of water works which will give employment to a great many hands this year, and put about $75,000 in circulation in our city.

The Gas Works is an old established concern, and affords an illumination superior to that of many larger cities.

The Daily DEMOCRAT justly comes under the head of our industries. It is a member

H. R. STEELE, Pres. N., R. R. & T. Ry.

of the associated press and gives the latest telegraphic news in time for breakfast every morning except Monday. It gives employment to about fifteen men.

The Tri-Weekly BANNER is another local industry and while only a yearling, is a

R. F. LEARNED, Pres. Natchez Cotton Mill.

sprightly child. It furnishes employment for eight or ten people.

That our people favor industrial ventures is evident from the fact that every dollar invested in those just enumerated is the money of Natchez people. But there are still many things needed which our people have not the

money at present to proceed with. To the people of the North therefore is this invitation extended "Come over into Macedonia and help us!"

OUR CHURCHES.

PRESBYTERIAN.

THE Presbyterian congregation at Natchez is a large and vigorous body. They have a spacious and elegant house of worship at the corner of Pearl and State

J. C. SCHWARTZ, Pres. Rosalie Cotton Mill.

streets, a chapel at the corner of Pearl and Washington streets, and a mission station on St. Catherine street. A Presbyterian element existed in this community prior to the

LOUIS BOTTO, Pres. Compress Co.

establishment of the Mississippi Territory in 1797, consisting of colonists of Scotch origin and from New England. They were formally organized into a church in 1817. The purpose to erect a place of worship had been formed as early as 1810, and was completed in 1815. The original structure was replaced in 1829 by a more imposing one, and this, in turn, was enlarged in 1851 into the dimensions and form in which the present stately edifice appears.

The number of enrolled communicants in this church is about 360. The pastor is the Rev. Joseph B. Stratton D. D., who commenced his ministry at this point and has been in office since December 31, 1843. Associated with him is a Bench of 9 Elders and a Board of 5 Deacons.

The constituency of the Presbyterian

THE METHODIST CHURCH.

THE introduction of Methodism in Natchez occurred in 1798, the same year in which United States authority was established here. Tobias Gibson, a South Carolinian, was the first minister, and Natchez was one of a large circuit of appointments which it became his duty to fill. He traveled on horseback or on foot and endured all the hardships incident to a new country, and succeeded in establishing in a few years such congregations that assistances was required to attend the work. This was furnished by volunteers from the army of willing workers educated

ST. MARY'S CATHEDRAL, NATCHEZ.

church has always included in it some of the best members of this community, and has furnished a succession of public spirited workers in every cause connected with the educational philanthropic and moral interests of the city. Its policy has been uniformly conservative, and its relation with other religious bodies have been maintained in a generous and fraternal spirit. The congregation is in all respects in a healthy and prosperous condition at the present time.

in the faith, and the results have been satisfactory in the extreme. Their system of changing ministers and the many excellent men who have been stationed here in consequence, render it impossible to go into details in this work, but that the church has has kept apace with others in the matter of successful work is evident in the splendid structure occupied by a large congregation, on the corner of Jefferson and Union streets, Wesley chapel, a less pretentious, but not less zealous church for the benefit of the factory operatives and citizens of the north-

ern portion of this city, and a commodious brick structure on Pine street, occupied by the colored Methodists. The membership of these churches is composed of some of our best people, both white and black and all visitors are cordially welcomed.

TRINITY EPISCOPAL CHURCH.

THE conception of old Trinity dates back to a dining at the hospitable board of the late Dr. Stephen Duncan, during the year 1821. Before many days the seed germinated and the organization was accomplished. The Rev. James Pilmore was the first rector, and began his ministry here on Sunday evening, May, 10, 1822, in the Presbyterian church.

WALL STREET BAPTIST CHURCH.

THE Wall Street Baptist Church is situated on the corner of State and Wall streets. This organization in Natchez is a half century old, the church being organized on the 11th of January 1837. Rev. Ashley Vaughan, a clergyman from one of the Northern States who came South in search of health, was its first Pastor. Their commodious church house was erected in 1851, and enlarged in 1857 to give seating capacity to the growing congregation. This church has at present about two hundred members, and is in a growing and encouraging condition. Within the last two years their house of worship has been beautified and furnished

L'EVEREUX HALL ORPHAN ASYLUM.

Soon after a subscription paper was started, for the purpose of securing aid to erect a church building, which was liberally signed, and early in May 1823 the edifice was ready for occupation. Alterations and improvements were made in 1838 and more recently, until now they have an elegant house of worship, at a cost of about $35,000. The Sunday-School Guild recently purchased a lot adjoining the one on which the church stands, and through the munificent liberality of one of the parishoners, a Sunday-School and Parish Building is to be erected this season, at a cost of over $10,000.

with modern appointments to make it attractive and to inspire devotion. Neither pains nor means have been spared by the congregation to put it in a condition to be at once abreast with the present demands of the church-going public and a Sabbath home where the humble may feel easy and the stranger find a welcome. Though the recent improvements have cost about $2500 the organization is out of debt, and the membership united for aggressive work in our growing city. The church has a live Sunday-School with one hundred and fifty scholars enrolled. For the last three years Rev. Z. T. Leavell has presided over the congregation as Pastor, and enjoins the full confidence and the hearty and united support of his people.

THE CATHOLIC CHURCH.

THE history of Catholicism in this section dates back to 1682. The notes of the progress of the church have been carefully kept and handed down to the people of the present day, and are very interesting. Natchez is the See of Mississippi, and Rt. Rev. F. Janssens is the present Bishop. He is a gentleman who rules his people by love, and he has won the esteem of members of all denominations, by his goodness.

The church has the most beautiful and commodious building in the city, and we believe in the entire South.

Saint Mary's Orphan Asylum, for girls, D'Evereux Hall an Orphan Asylum for boys, the Cathedral school, and St. Joseph's school are all under the auspices of the church and are most successful institutions.

There is no ill feeling between them and the Protestants such as unfortunately exists in some places, but all work hand in hand to accomplish good.

COTTON AND MERCHANTS EXCHANGE.

ON May 26, 1886, our business men, realizing the benefits to be derived from co-operative organization, secured a charter from the State of Mississippi and established "The Natchez Cotton and Mer-

J. N. CARPENTER, Pres. Cotton Exchange.

chants Exchange," officered by the following leading business men: Joseph N. Carpenter, President; A. G. Campbell, Vice-President; Simon Mayer, Secretary; Theo. V. Wensel, Treasurer. The Board of Directors are, Chas. T. Chamberlain, Geo. T. Payne, F. A. Dicks, Henry Frank and Isaac Lowenburg.

Their headquarters are fitted up in modest but comfortable style at the corner of Main and Commerce streets, the heart of the city, and there they receive daily every half hour the market reports of the world, which are posted on the board for the edification of members.

Their organization and the building of our

MAJ. JOHN RAWLE.

large cotton compress last year brought a flood of cotton buyers, who competed successfully with New Orleans, and induced an increase in cotton receipts of over 20,000 bales.

The expenses of the institution are light and the benefits have proven so great, with such prospects of even a better future, that it is no longer an experiment but is one of the solidest organization in the city.

THE NATCHEZ CLUB.

THIS social organization, was permanently instituted on March 5th 1883, by election of L. G. Aldrich, President; John Rawle, Vice-President; Richard Holmes, Secretary and Treasurer, who have continued to fill same position by annual election.

The club embraces in its membership about seventy-five citizens from the leading representatives of its various trades and professions.

Their rooms are centrally located with pleasing inner and outer surroundings, and afford agreeable relaxation from the cares and toils of business, by presenting to its members, innocent amusement as well as an extensive collection of daily weekly and month-

At 77 Main Street, corner of Main and Pearl, will be found the vast establishment of A. Bahin. The store is 160 feet deep, two stories high, and is well stocked with Dry Goods, Shoes, Hats, Notions and Millinery Goods, both wholesale and retail.

This establishment is a sample of what uprightness and application to business will do. Mr. Bahin came to Natchez at the age of eight years, in 1850. After the war he found himself an orphan, without a cent.

After clerking a few years he started in business with eight hundred dollars, and now finds himself one of the leading merchants, doing a large business.

Though surprising to some, the headway he made in business is the natural consequence of being surrounded by a fine country both in Mississippi and Louisiana—lands that are capable of smiling abundant success to farmer and merchant alike.

We commend the public at home and abroad to this wide-awake firm for goods in his line. And for good, honest goods, and good value for price, he cannot be excelled.

ly publication, from the leading journals of this country and England.

Its hospitality to visiting strangers is in keeping with the world renowned reputation of the city whose name it bears.

REAL ESTATE AND RENTS.

NATCHEZ is on a boom, and has been for several years—not a fictitious boom gotten up by big mineral excitements, but a steady natural improvement, caused by the outside world discovering that on the bluffs overlooking the great Mississippi, stands a beautiful city just far enough south for a pleasant home, just high enough to insure health, and surrounded by a fertile country

Dixon Brothers' Store and Glass Works.

which insures good living. There are a few people here, who, in a spirit of love and vention for the old homestead have placed a fictitious price on their land, but there is plenty of land to be had at a convenient distance from the city at from $3 to $20 per acre, and improved land at that. Town lots can be purchased on good terms at reasonable prices.

Rents for dwellings in Natchez, are like they are in other growing cities, rather high ; houses of four to five rooms near the center of the city rent for about $20 per month with a proportionate increase in houses with more rooms. The general expenses of living, fuel etc., are not so great as in the north and east, which I think more than makes up the difference in rents.

ADAMS COUNTY.

BY ALLISON H. FOSTER.

TO write of Adams county, its history of the past, its present activity and worth and its future prospects of greater wealth and grandeur, is a pleasant duty.

In the distant past, when the stillness of nature was only broken by the weird chant,

Allison H. Foster, Chancery Clerk of County.

or echoing, resounding whoop of the red man, as he roamed at will over the hills and valleys of our country ; or when a softer spirit moved him, to woo, win and wed, the dusky maiden of the forest, under the shade of the majestic oak, in whose enfolding branches nestled the mistletoe, an allwise Deity, and

James W. Lambert, Sheriff.

bounteous nature, had generously endowed this favored spot, with many choice gifts.

Advancing civilization, in its many and just conquests, long since forced the Indian with his untutored mind, to seek shelter, and erect his wigwam to the far west, and nearer the setting sun. "White Apple Village," in this county ; the once cherished home of mighty chiefs and tribes; is now traced and recognized only. by the peaceful pursuits of the sturdy yeoman, as he follows the plow, and in due season gathers in the fruits, the natural reward of his honest labor.

Adams county, fronts nearly one hundred miles, on the Mississippi river. The soil is alluvial, and, where not permitted, with constant tillage and without return to the soil to become worn and thin. is exceedingly

Hon. O. N. Wilds, Pres. Board of Supervisors

rich and productive. The famous valley of the Nile is no richer in soil, than the bottom lands of Adams county.

The topography of our country is varied and in places rolling, while in others we find plateaus, and rising or hilly ground. The chief product of our county is cotton; but

J. C. Stowers, Member Board of Supervisors

four other crops can be raised annually on the same ground. There is not an acre of land in the county, if properly cultivated, that will not return annually a cash value of

fifty dollars ; and this land can now be purchased from $2 oo to $20 per acre.

The climate here is delightful. trees in foliage and flowers blooming in profusion in the months of February and March. Think of it. oh, denizens of the congealed north and east, and envy must for a time enthrone itself within your breasts. We, contemplate you, as snowed in, ice bound, cold and freezing, while we, with doors and win-

H. B. Vaughan, Member Board of Supervisors

dows open are inhaling the perfume of budding flowers, and listening to the songs of the mocking bird.

Adams county invites you to join, in the triumphal march of the emancipated New South. Her people are intelligent, courteous, industrious and refined, and all who come to

J. H. Rowan, Member Board of Supervisors

partake of her fortunes will be met with cordial greetings and neither asked or influenced concerning their political or religious fealty or allegiance. Good men, and good

Residence of J. R. Kirkpatrick, Natchez.

"Montaigne," Residence of Gen. W. T. Martin, Natchez Suburbs.

"D'Evereux," Property of Miss M. S. Martin, Natchez Suburbs.

Residence of Alderman Geo. T. Rehn, Natchez.

citizens alone, are wanted, and to such, we have abundant room, and a hearty, generous, and honest welcome.

The early boyhood days of the writer having been spent in the place of his nativity, the old "Granite" State, and therefore being somewhat familiar with the mode of farming and customs of the people both North and South, is constrained to assert that the intelligent, frugal, industrious North-

C. L. Tillman, Treasurer.

ern farmer, if transplanted to this portion of the South, and exercising here like habits of thrift, industry and economy as at the North, would, in the brief period of ten years, or less, awake to the pleasing fact that his possessions were abundantly sufficient to enable

Walter McCrea, Deputy Clerk.

him to enjoy the rest of his days independent of manual labor for a support.

No better field presents itself for the establishment of manufactories, and especially of wood-work, than Natchez and Adams

county, as timber of the best quality and of many species abounds in almost endless quantity, right at our doors.

The future of Natchez and Adams county is assured and bright, and chief among the jewels that adorn and crown them is the love of country, confidence and determination within the hearts of the good people to bend every energy to the advancement and weal of both. Southward the "Star of Empire"

John Harper, Deputy Sheriff.

is at last seen; it is making rapid progress in this direction, and is received by the New South with open arms, brave, honest and manly hearts, and welcome, thrice welcome to our shores.

Lands here are now cheap, but are fast becoming equalized in value, with that in other portions of our common country.

Adams county invites a fair, yes, critical

Salvo & Berdon's Block, Natchez.

inspection of the many advantages she presents to those seeking homes in the South, or safe and profitable investments; and conscious she is that the verdict of "the stranger within our gates" will not be adverse to her present worth or future greatness.

Far be it from me to misrepresent; consequently I affirm that "milk and honey" are only obtained here, as the certain, just, and merited reward, for manly enterprise devotion to duty, and honest industry. Human nature, here, is compassed with foibles and frailties, common to mankind, and is no nearer Divine than at the North. If one here, were to revile, malign or traduce the names or memory of Generals Lee or Jackson, the offender would instantly regret that he were not possessed of the strength of Sampson and science of Sullivan, with which to defend his unsavory person. I imagine, the spirit of human nature and justice would obtain in the

COUNTY BOARD OF SUPERVISORS.

IT is very gratifying to us, to write of the conservative, wide, and intelligent management of county affairs, by our Board of Supervisors.

For some years after the war, things obtained, under the chaotic condition of our county then existing, that were neither equitable; just, or complimentary to our ability, and inalienable right, of self government. Happily, those things are of the past. In 1875 the good citizens of our county, irrespective of party or color, united, and placed in power, men of well known ability and integrity, and men who regarded the county's in-

Bluff City Railway Incline to the Hill Tops.

North, were contumely or malevolence spoken against the honored names or memory of President Lincoln or General Grant. Sectionalism here, is buried in the dark gloom of the past, and its phantom, is not permitted to cross or shadow our pathway. May the day soon come when deriding allusions to the Nations honored dead, whether of the blue or gray and wheresoever in our blessed and united country made, shall be quickly, spontaneously and patriotically denounced and resented. Such, I believe, is now, the honest sentiment, and patriotism, that, unbidden, wells up from the hearts of a brave, united and devoted people.

terests as their own. Results plainly demonstrate the wisdom of the people's choice. From the legacy of debt, profligacy, and burdensome taxation handed down, our Board of Supervisors, have so eminently managed the people's trust, confided to their care, that long years ago, order from chaos, economy from profligacy, and minimum taxation from that bordering upon absolute confiscation, has pre-eminently marked their faithful, and oft-times self-sacrificing labors.

Some changes in the Board that first entered official life in January 1876, have, by death, resignation and retirement been made; but the people feel justly proud of the good work of all that have been connected with it

during that period. With good roads, bridges, and low taxation, our people are contented and happy.

The gentlemen composing our Board of Supervisors, are the Hon. Oliver N. Wilds, President; Jas. H. Rowan, H. B. Vaughan Jno. C. Stowers and A. P. Williams. Mr. Wilds has been on the Board twelve, Mr. Rowan ten, and the others a lesser number of years. Mr. Williams is a colored man.

The names of other members during said period, and not now connected with the Board,

vehicle drawn by two horses or other animals, with one or more passengers, $8 00.

For the use of any Hack or vehicle, with one or more passengers, with the privilege of going from place to place, and stopping as often as may be requested, for the first hour, $2 00.

For each succeeding hour, $1 00.

For attending funerals, $3 00.

The following rates shall be charged by the owner or driver of any wagon for the transportation of baggage, as follows, viz·

Union School, (Colored), Natchez,

are the Hon. T. C. Pollock (deceased) late President, and Geo. M. Marshall, Daniel F. Ashford, and Alex Smart, (also a colored man.) To the names, memory and work of all and to our present Board, the welcome plaudit goes out: "Well done thou good and faithful servants."

HACK RATES.

CITY ORDINANCE.

For conveying a passenger not exceeding one mile, 50 cts.

For conveying a passenger over one mile, 75 cts.

After 10 o'lock at night, double rates.

For use by the day of any Hack or other

For transporting each and every trunk, not exceeding one mile, 25 cts.

For transporting each and every trunk any distance over one mile, 50 cts.

☞ Hack owners or drivers are required to keep these rules posted in a conspicuous place within their vehicles.

All hotels and boarding houses are within a mile of steamboat landings and depots.

TRUCK FARMING AND GARDENING.

THE possibilities in this branch of agriculture are without limit; the local market is good and the shipping facilities by river and rail are excellent. The following extract from a local paper will best illustrate the advantages offered by our climate Rose potatoes on a piece of land near town, about one hundred and fifty feet square, from which he gathered twenty-five barrels of as fine potatoes as can be produced anywhere. The barrels used by him held three bushels, and putting the price at one dollar per bushel which can readily be realized, the yield brings him seventy-five dollars. The cost of pro-

Presbyterian Church, Natchez.

and soil.

" An instance of the profitable returns from truck farming and rotation of crops has been brought to our notice recently. Mr. Isaac Friedler made a planting in January of Early ducing, including the price of the potatoes planted, did not exceed five dollars, and since taking off the crop in April, he has planted the same ground in cotton, and will, with favorable seasons, make a full crop."—Con-

Residence of John A. Dicks, Natchez.

Residence of A. C. Britton, Banker, Natchez.

"Dunleith," Suburban Residence of J. N. Carpenter.

Chamberlain & Paterson's Block.

M. Neihysel's Confectionery.

cordia, (La.) Sentinel, May 7.

The above is not a rare case of production but was the result of only moderate attention; and the same conditions will apply to any other crop planted in the garden or truck patch.

A friend, who lives in the southern part of this county, brought the writer a basket of strawberries on the first of May, which had been hurriedly picked, just before starting to the city, without sorting for large ones, and nine of them filled a pint measure. The gentleman informed us that he had paid no special attention to his plants farther than to get good ones and protect them from weeds and grass.

Blackberries and dew berries grow wild in

FARMS AND FARMING.

THE variety of opportunities and advantages offered by this country is so great that it is almost impossible to give a coherent idea of them in a work like this, but if, by enumerating a few, an investigation of the claims of the South can be secured, we have nothing to fear for our future.

The topography of the country is very similar to that in Northern Indiana and Central Ohio. It is well drained, well watered and and the soil is a rich alluvial deposit of wonderful depth and strength, and is well adapted for any crops raised in the North, East or West. The warm winters are not good for

Residence Alderman L. G. Aldrich, Natchez.

almost inexhaustible quantities, and have been selling on the streets during the past two months at ten cents per gallon.

Sweet potatoes, tomatoes, peas, beans, etc., are in their natural element here, and from two to four finely matured crops ars produced on the same ground every season.

Help is cheap and general expenses are light, while the gardener has the fixing of his own prices for his products, for, if he cannot get his prices here, he can conveniently ship to greater markets.

fall wheat, but aside from that any crop can be profitably cultivated. Mississippi produced last year 25,765,000 bushels of corn 3,962,-000 bushels of oats, 173,000 bushels of wheat, hundreds of thousands of tons of timothy, clover and other grasses, all grasses thrive well here, and the main question with the farmers has been to discover which contains the greatest nutriment. The following comparative analysis is by Prof Phares of one of Mississippi's agricultural colleges:

Japan Clover (Lespedeza Striata) Hay
     71.85 per cent nutriment.
Red Clover Hay 57. " " "
Orchard Grass 52. " " "

Pea	56.	"	"	"
Vetches	49.	"	"	"
Timothy	48.50.	"	"	"
Blue Grass	48.	"	"	"

In addition to being the most nutritious, the Lespedeza is considered the strongest fertilzer known, and a vigorous, hearty plant, which yields well in either wet or dry seasons.

The system of farming, as followed by the darkies, has gotton this country into bad repute as far as agriculture goes, but a visit and personal inspection by the average Northern farmer will convince him of the great error. Take, for instance, our short winters, instead of having to feed stock seven or eight

FRUIT CULTURE.

IN days gone by no country was more justly celebrated for its fine fruit than South-West Mississippi. During the war the orchards were neglected and many were totally obliterated from the face of the earth, and when peace once more reigned the people had to plant something that promised quicker returns than fruit trees. After a few years however, they began to set out young trees, and now there are to be found many nice orchards of apples, peaches, pears, plums, quinces, apricots, pumegranates, olives, figs, pecans, grapes, etc., but there is room for

Opera House, Natchez.

months on grain and hay, we feed one month on hay, and many do not feed at all. Our summers are long but not excessively hot, there is a pleasant gulf breeze at times and the nights are almost invariably cool and delightful. Our altitude is such that malaria is unknown. The price of our land is low, from three to twenty dollars per acre and good roads all the year round by which to reach it. Our educational and religious facilities are old established. Our people are not only willing, but anxious for thrifty farmers to come among them, and by these presents do guarantee them as good treatment and as good a living, easier made than in the much boomed West.

many more and a profitable return to their owners for the trouble of planting. All fruit ripens early and there is a fortune in a very few years to the man who ships to the North. It is a mistaken idea that the majority of the Northern people have about this as a fruit country. Fresh figs are the only fruit which can not be shipped as they come from the tree, in that regard they are like a persimmon and must be dried before shipment. The fig is considered the most wholesome of fruits, one can eat all he wants without the slightest danger, and as they grow so abundantly here, we guarantee any and all who come here in June and July all they can eat fresh from the trees, or with cream and sugar, for breakfast, they cannot fail to give even a dyspeptic an appetite, and aid in restoring his health and consequently his good nature.

Fruit begins to ripen about the first of April, and continues until late in the fall, and with anything like proper care the little enemies, so commonly known in the North are entirely avoided here.

Melons, we need not mention for the reason that the darkie, the mule and the melon are so thoroughly associated in the mind of the Northern people that where one exists they know the others certainly do, and also for the reason that if we were to tell the whole truth you wouldn't believe it ; so we send you this invitation to come and see for yourselves.

OUR HEALTH.

BY J. C. FRENCH, M. D.

THE object of this article is to set forth the advantages of the City of Natchez and County of Adams as health and pleasure resorts at all seasons of the year. It is written at the request of the pub-

DR. J. C. FRENCH.

lisher of this work, and in answer to many letters received by the writer from friends and acquaintances in Southeastern Indiana and Ohio.

My personal experience in this country is as follows : On November 10, 1885, I, with my family, landed in Natchez, leaving our old home, (Greensburg, Ind.,) contrary to the advice of our relatives and friends, who told us that we Northern people would not be welcome here, that we would be ostracised from society, that no one would want my professional services, that we would have malaria and yellow fever and die ; that Northern people could not live in this climate, etc. During my residence of about

three years in Natchez, I have found my friends were mistaken. In the first place we were welcomed by a people than whom there are no more sociable, hospitable, sympathizing and generous anywhere ; they ever have a hearty welcome for all good citizens.

Now about our health: The day we left Indiana my wife weighed 116 pounds ; to-day she weighs 140 pounds. During the cold, damp winter season in Indiana, she had a continuous, distressing cough ; she now has no cough either winter or summer, and enjoys perfect health. My weight was 135 pounds ; to-day I "knock the beam" at 170 pounds. My two children, as well as Mrs. French and myself, have never been sick a day. We are living monuments to the virtue of the climate of Natchez. The foregoing is a true statement of facts, and I hope will convince some of their mistaken opinion of this country.

Natchez, destined to be the metropolis of this section of the country, is a live city of magnificent expectations and over 11,000 inhabitants. It is a well-known settled principle

CAPT. J. M. BOWEN, Coal Dealer.

of economy, that in order to secure the permanent growth of a city, every citizen and every department of the city's government should work together in perfect harmony and union. This principle has been enforced here, and the existing circumstances are all favorable to a growing and substantial boom.

Natchez is recorded the second healthiest city in the United States—New Haven, Connecticut, taking first honors.

What makes it so healthy? First, its high elevation ; second, its natural drainage ; third, its spring-like climate ; fourth, its pure drinking water. These four advantages we will consider separately and leave you to compare with other places.

Its High Elevation—Many people in the North and Northwest have the opinion that all the territory south of Mason & Dixon's line is a breeder and feeder of malaria. This is as true of a portion of the South as it is of the Wabash section of Indiana. The swamp country of Mississippi and Louisiana is full of malaria at certain seasons of the year, and it is very hazardous for a person not acclimated, to even visit that section during such periods. The only malarial deseases Natchez physicians have to contend with are in people from the swamp, who come over to the hills annually for medical treatment, and such cases are almost invariably successfully coped with. The germs of malarial poison travel to a hight of about 60 feet and

WM. STEITENROTH, Architect.

are then dissipated. The country on the North, East and South sides of the City of Natchez is hilly, and Natchez is justly called the "Bluff City.," Our altitude is such that we constantly enjoy cool, refreshing breezes from the Gulf, making the evenings and nights very pleasant even in midsummer.

Natural Drainage—The centre and sidewalks of each street are about two feet higher than the gutters on either side, with a natural decline toward the river, and all water is carried at once to that stream. Stagnant water ponds are as much unknown to Natchez as are ice and snow in winter. After the heaviest rainfall twenty-four hours, the streets are dry. No artificial means could improve our natural drainage.

Its Spring-like Climate—Here the sunshine is an every day occurrence. It is neither too hot nor too cold, the thermometer rarely going above 90 degrees in Summer and never below zero in winter, making the dry, non-poisonous atmosphere so essentially necessary to the relief and cure of those suffering with pulmonary and bronchial diseases. Con-

sumptives, from the cold Northwestern climate, can, in many instances, be cured, and always have life prolonged by a residence in this climate. Consumption seldom originates here, except among the negro population, and then the cause can invariably be traced to neglect and improper care.

Our Pure Drinking water—It is well known that cholera and kindred diseases are invariably traced to impure water, Rainwater, the purest of all waters, is used by every family in this city. Large and carefully constructed cisterns are built, and are filled during our rainy or winter season with a supply sufficient to last through the summer.

A visit to our city and an investigation of its claims cannot fail to satisfy the most skeptical.

LIVE STOCK.

TO the stock farmer this country offers extraordinary inducements over any other. First, the climate; second, the luxuriant pasture; third, the fine water; fourth, the market; fifth, the slight cost of raising an animal.

The even temperature of Southwest Mississippi is destined to be her crowning glory, for with it come all the other blessings: health, wealth and happiness. A few days in each winter the temperature falls to about 15 degrees above zero, and a very few in summer it is above 90.

Our land is splendidly adapted to meadow and pasture grasses, which grow with such rapidity that close-cropping animals, like sheep, cannot keep them down.

Fine water, one of the great essentials for stock raising, is here in abundance, in wells, cisterns and running streams.

The market facilities are of the very best, with plenty of rail and river facilities to insure low freight rates.

With all the above points settled, the general cost of raising stock is reduced to the minimum. In the North and West I believe the cost for grain to feed each head of cattle through a winter is about $25. Here no grain is fed at all. There are two or three breeders of fine cattle and horses near this city, and in February this year I visited their farms and found every animal sleek and fat, and was informed they had never seen any grain in their troughs in their lives—nothing but the rich, juicy hay, produced right on the farms.

For hogs there is no better place in the

"Elmscourt," Residence of the Merrills, Natchez Suburbs.

Residence of Henry Frank, Natchez.

Natchez Cotton Mills, Main Building.

St. Mary's Orphan Asylum, Natchez.

world. All the ground crops that are raised anywhere grow abundantly here, and the mast includes acorns, beech-nuts and other fattening tree fruits.

Sheep are a remarkable success here. The writer spent the greater part of his life in the North, and knows the anxiety with which the farmer cares for his sheep; and to be a successful sheep farmer there requires capital with which to house them properly, for, when a sheep makes up his mind that he is tired of bad weather, he is going to die, and it is useless to try to save him. Here, the climate is especially suited to them; all the shelter they care for is given by a rick of corn fodder for them to pass under and browse at until a cold rain is over. Only once in about seven years do we have snow, and there never has been more than one snow storm during a winter, and that does not last two days.

Considerable attention is now being devoted to fine breeds of cattle, and in every instance those brought from the North have been improved. The natives here read with astonishment last winter, the telegrams from the West telling of cattle perishing in the storms. They cannot conceive how the weather can be severe enough to kill stock, and yet stockmen be induced to remain in that country.

Fine horses are, and always have been the pride of Southern people, and although they are pretty severe in their usage sometimes, it is a common thing to see a span of high-headed twenty-year-olds dashing along the streets like colts.

Everything about this country is conducive to long life to both man and beast, and the only reason it has not been filled up long ago is that the people of the North have not known its value.

OUR MILITIA.

NATCHEZ has always been justly proud of her soldiers. She encourages military organization. not for warlike purposes, but because it brings the young men together socially and the drills develope their muscles and make them better men physically. We will not attempt the early history of the companies here, but will speak briefly of each to-day.

Adams Light infantry was organized in 1876 and is composed mainly of veterans of the recent war. Captain T. Otis Baker, an old veteran and thoroughly accomplished drillmaster, is annually re-elected chief officer;

the company have a nicely furnished armory, and are among the fixtures of the city.

The Natchez Fencibles claim the honor of being the oldest military company in the city. The present company is composed of

Capt. F. J. V. LeCand.

young men whose fathers made its name famous in years gone by. Capt. Fred. J. V. LeCand, a gentleman of well-known military ability, and also a veteran, has command.

The memory of the valiant deeds of their ancestors inspired the organization of the Natchez Rifles about a year ago, and through the persistent drilling of their enthusiastic captain, Brinton B Davis, they have become so

Capt. Brinton B. Davis.

perfect in the tactics that they will soon challenge the Mobile company, who won the first prize at the national drill in May last, and they undoubtedly have a fair prospect of a successful competition.

SECRET SOCIETIES.

OUR city has a representative organization of almost every fraternity in existence: Masons, Odd Fellows, Knights of Pythias, Knights of Honor, Knights of Labor, Catholic societies, Jewish societies,

Grand Master Mason E. G. DeLap.

Colored societies, all in a flourishing condition. Some of our citizens have been honored by their brethren of the Grand Lodges of the State: the present Grand Master Mason and the Grand High Priest of Royal Arch Masons, are Natchez business men. In the

Grand High Priest C. T. Chamberlain.

Jewish and Catholic circles many of our citizens are honored with high positions.

A sketch of each of the lodges here would be interesting to fraternities generally but limited space forbids it in this work.

DON'T.

DON'T judge the South by merely viewing it from a flying railroad train. If you do you will form a poor opinion every time. Remember that Mississippi passed through a war which left few houses and

J. C. Schwartz' Block.

no fences standing; that Mississippi is 6,000 square miles larger than Ohio, and has only one-third as many inhabitants, half of whom are shiftless negroes, who do not aspire to own land, and who are ignorant of all proper means of cultivating it if they did own it.

Rumble & Wensel's Block.

Stop at our towns; talk to our people; drive out and examine the land; ask how long it has been used without fertilizer, and what it is now producing. Observe the way it is tilled, and you will as surely come to the conclusion that you can find no better place to cast your lot.

HUNTING AND FISHING.

BY JOHN F. JENKINS.

WHILE the energies of our people are bent toward the advancement of their manufacturing and agricultural interests; and while the rewards which have accrued to those who first launched the manfacturing enterprises are exciting further emulation in these directions, still there are moments spared from the press of business by many of our citizens to indulge in the healthful and manly exercise of field sports, which the near country around furnishes in attractive abundance and variety.

Within a radius of twenty miles around Natchez the sportsman can find deer, bear, wild turkeys and quail in abundance; and in their proper season, ducks, snipe and woodcock.

DEER—The popular mode of hunting deer in this section is to drive them with hounds, and take stands for them in the runways. Good deer-hunting of this sort can be had in St. Catherine's swamps, six miles from Natchez; also near Fairchild's Island, thirteen miles distant, and in the Homochitto swamps, twenty miles away; but the best deer-hunting, perhaps, in America, is to be found on Ben's Lake, in the edge of Catahoula Parish, Louisiana, midway between the Tensas and Ouachita rivers, and the distance from Natchez is only twenty-eight miles. It is easy of access by wagon, or by rail and steamer. The species of deer in this section are the common Virginia deer. The buck with four or five points on his horns often nets 200 to 250 pounds, and have been known to reach 300 pounds.

BEAR—The species of bear is the common black fellow. He is found in great abundance on Turtle lake, about thirteen miles from Natchez, and is plentiful all over Concordia parish. Our bear generally net about 250 to 300 pounds, when full grown. They are always hunted with dogs.

WILD TURKEYS—Are found in almost every direction from Natchez. Their favorite resorts are Big Oak Ridge, in St. Catherine Swamp, and in the Homochitto swamp. They are most commonly hunted in the months of March and April, when they are mating. Wild turkey gobblers often attain a weight of 20 pounds. Hunting turkeys is exciting sport, and many sportsmen, among them the writer, derive greater satisfaction from the capture of a twenty-pound gobbler with his eighteen-inch beard, than from kill-

ing a two-hundred-pound buck with six points on his antlers.

QUAIL OR PARTRIDGE.—Of all the field sports in this vicinity quail shooting is the pursuit that has the most devotees. It is the one that is easiest to reach and is certain to put game in the bag in the shortest time. The very best localities near Natchez for this game are Stanton Station, on the "Little J." railroad, "Beverly" plantation in Second Creek bottom and others, all within twelve miles of the city.

DUCKS.—In the middle of November the ducks begin to arrive and afford fine sport until January. We have the Mallard and Teal in great abundance. There are many fine resorts for this bird, but the favorite one is Homochitto swamp, because of the growth of wild celery, which has a great attraction for them and gives their flesh a most delicious flavor.

SNIPE—Good snipe hunting can be had in the months of February and March at Giles' swamp, at "Beverly" and "Frogmore" plantations. On the latter place they are in great abundance.

FISH.—There are many fine fish in our neighboring lakes. Our great game fish are the green trout and the bar fish or striped bass. The best bait for the trout is a small minnow, while the bar fish is readily taken with shrimp. The trout weighs from one to eight pounds, and the bar fish from one to four pounds.

A Few Bags That Have Been Made.— Near Ben's lake, a party of hunters killed 1200 pounds of venison on a single hunt.

In quail shooting the average hunter bags about twenty birds per day; but a bag of 75 birds was made in one day on "Beverly" plantation.

The biggest bags of birds have been made on Sicily Island, where 90 birds per diem to the man is not considered extraordinary.

At Gaillard's lake a party of four hunters killed in one day two hundred and three Mallard ducks. One of the party, the president of the Gaillard Sporting Club, scoring sixty-five Mallards in three hours snooting.

Bags of two hundred snipe to two hunters have been made in one day.

One of the best bags known to the writer was made by a party of three sportsmen in the vicinity of Gaillord's lake, when, in two days they had 21 quail, 15 snipe, 5 woodcock, 35 green-winged Teal, 10 Mallards and 1 deer.

One of the recorded fish frys took place at Old River cut off, when 475 bar fish were taken with rod and line from 5 to 9 o'clock a. m., by eight fishermen.

GAME LAWS. ETC.

The game laws of this county have recently been amended so as to prohibit all hunting of every species of game from March 15 to November 1, of each year. This is a strict law and no doubt should be modified as to some varieties of game. But the idea is that if there are different dates for different game, pot hunters will take advantage of it to destroy some game whose period for being hunted had expired.

Our farmers and planters as a rule make no objection to sportsmen hunting on their lands, and where there is an exceptional case of "posting" the lands, a personal application readily obtains the desired permission.

One of the chief recommendations that Natchez and vicinity offer to the zealous sportsman is its magnificent climate. During the shooting season, from November to March, there are only a few days when the weather is at all bitter, say from January 1 to 15, the average temperature for the balance of the shooting season ranging from 40 to 64 degrees Fahrenheit, so the sportsman can utilize almost the whole of the shooting season without that strain upon the health which extremes of temperature in many other places so often exerts.

The object in sending out this book is to let the world know what we have here, and I would say to visitors after you have examined our agricultural and industrial resources come and take a hunt with us, and we will show you that in addition to the other things we have hunting and fishing second to no place in America.

LAWS OF MISSISSIPPI.

THERE is exempt from seizure and sale, under execution or attachment, in favor of each head of a family or housekeeper in this State, the following property, to-wit : Two work-horses or mules or one yoke oxen, two cows and calves, five head of stock hogs and five sheep, one hundred and fifty bushels of corn, ten bushels of wheat or rice, two hundred pounds of pork or bacon or other meat, one cart or wagon not to exceed one hundred dollars in value, household and kitchen funiture to be selected by the debtor not to exceed one hundred dollars in value, three hundred bundles of fodder, one sewing

machine, and all colts under three years old raised in this State by the debtor, and the wages of every laborer or mechanic to the amount of one hundred dollars. The following property is likewise exempt in the hands of the persons, named, viz : The tools of a mechanic necessary in carrying on his trade, the agricultural implements of a farmer necessary for two male laborers. the implements of a laborer necessary in his usual employment, the books of a student required for the completion of his education, the wearing apparel of every person, the libraries of licensed attorneys at law, practicing physicians and ministers of the gospel not exceeding two hundred and fifty dollars in value ; also the instruments of surgeons and dentists used in their profession not exceeding two hundred and fifty dollars in value, the arms and accoutrements of each person of the militia of the State, and all globes, books and maps used by teachers of schools, academies and colleges. That every citizen of this State, male or female, being a householder and having a family, shall be entitled to hold, exempt from seizure or sale under execution or attachment, the land and buildings owned and occupied as a residence by such debtor, provided the quantity of land shall not exceed one hundred and sixty acres nor the value thereof, inclusive of improvements, the sum of two thousand dollars. The Legislature of the State has passed a law "exempting from taxation for ten years the machinery used for the manufacture of cotton and woolen goods, yarns and fabrics composed of these or other materials, or for the manufacture of agricultural implements and machinery.

Meteodist Episcopal Church, Natchez.

Residence of Dr. S. Kelly, Natchez.

R. F. Learned's Saw Mill.

Natchez College, (Colored.)